The LAST FIREHAWK

The Secret Maze

by
Katrina Charman

D0951653

The LAST FIREHAWK

Read All the Books

1. The Last Firehawk: The Ember Stone

2. The Last Firehawk: The Crystal Caverns

3. The Last Firehawk: The Whispering Oak

4. The Last Firehawk: Lullaby Lake

5. The Last Firehawk: The Shadowlands

6. The Last Firehawk: The Battle for Perodia

7. The Last Firehawk: The Cloud Kingdom

8. The Last Firehawk: The Silver Swamp

9. The Last Firehawk: The Golden Temple

10. The Last Firehawk: The Secret Maze

Table of Contents

~~~

For Brick, Piper, and Riley. —KC

Copyright © 2021 by Katrina Charman
Illustrations copyright © 2021 by Scholastic Inc.

All rights reserved. Published by Scholastic Inc., *Publishers since 1920.*
SCHOLASTIC, BRANCHES, and associated logos are trademarks and/or registered trademarks of Scholastic Inc.

The publisher does not have any control over and does not assume any responsibility for author or third-party websites or their content.

No part of this publication may be reproduced, stored in a retrieval system, or transmitted in any form or by any means, electronic, mechanical, photocopying, recording, or otherwise, without written permission of the publisher. For information regarding permission, write to Scholastic Inc., Attention: Permissions Department, 557 Broadway, New York, NY 10012.

This book is a work of fiction. Names, characters, places, and incidents are either the product of the author's imagination or are used fictitiously, and any resemblance to actual persons, living or dead, business establishments, events, or locales is entirely coincidental.

Library of Congress Cataloging-in-Publication Data

Names: Charman, Katrina, author. | Tondora, Judit, illustrator. | Charman, Katrina. Last firehawk; 10. Title: The secret maze / by Katrina Charman ; [illustrated by Judit Tondora]

Description: First edition. | New York : Branches/Scholastic Inc., 2021. Series: The last firehawk ; 10 | Summary: Now that Tag and Skyla have found Blaze's firehawk family they would like to return home to Perodia, even if it means leaving their friend behind; but in order to find the magic that will open a new portal they must first brave a mysterious underground maze where the walls are constantly shifting—and when they do find their way home there is a deadly surprise waiting for them.

Identifiers: LCCN 2020048388 | ISBN 9781338565379 (paperback) | ISBN 9781338565386 (library binding) | ISBN 9781338565393 (ebook)

Subjects: LCSH: Owls—Juvenile fiction. | Squirrels—Juvenile fiction. | Animals, Mythical—Juvenile fiction. | Magic—Juvenile fiction. | Labyrinths—Juvenile fiction. | Adventure stories. | CYAC: Owls—Fiction. | Squirrels—Fiction. | Animals, Mythical—Fiction. | Magic—Fiction. | Adventure and adventurers—Fiction. | Fantasy. | LCGFT: Action and adventure fiction. | Fantasy fiction.

Classification: LCC PZ7.1.C495 Se 2021 | DDC 823.92 [Fic]—dc23

LC record available at https://lccn.loc.gov/2020048388

10 9 8 7 6 5 4 3 2 1   21 22 23 24 25

Printed in China   62

First edition, November 2021
Illustrated by Judit Tondora
Edited by Rachel Matson
Book design by Jaime Lucero

~ INTRODUCTION ~

Tag, a small barn owl, and his friends
Skyla, a squirrel, and Blaze, a firehawk, have
journeyed through the Cloud Kingdom. They
traveled with the help of Claw, who says he is the twin
brother of the evil vulture named Thorn. Together
they opened a portal using the magical Ember Stone
and three golden feathers. The portal took them to
the Land of the Firehawks, where Blaze was finally
reunited with her mother, Talia, and the other
firehawks. Now that Blaze has found her home, Tag
and Skyla must prepare to say goodbye to their friend.
But it's not going to be easy for them to return home.

The golden feathers were lost in the Cloud
Kingdom, and without another powerful magical
object, Tag, Skyla, and Claw are unable to make
a portal home to Perodia. They will have to work
together to find a new magical object in the Land
of the Firehawks. Otherwise these friends may never
see their home again.

The adventure continues . . .

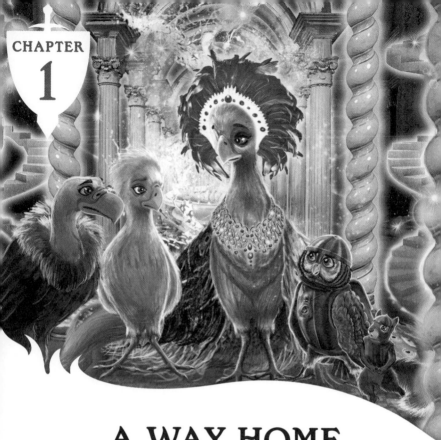

A WAY HOME

Tag, Skyla, Blaze, Claw, and Talia stood inside the firehawks' Golden Temple. The temple was beautiful. It had high ceilings, shiny golden pillars, and fountains that sparkled with rainbow-colored water.

"There must be a way we can go home," Skyla said, then sighed. Her bushy tail flicked back and forth. "The Land of the Firehawks is amazing, but I want to go back to Perodia."

Tag nodded sadly. "But how? We lost the golden feathers. And the Ember Stone alone is not strong enough to open a portal."

He remembered how they had used the golden feathers and the Ember Stone together to open portals to the Cloud Kingdom and to the Land of the Firehawks.

"We need to find a powerful magical object to open a portal," Blaze said.

"This land is full of magic," Claw said. "There must be one here somewhere."

Tag sighed. "Grey would know what to do," he said. He wished the leader of the Owls of Valor was there with them. "Or he could find the answer in one of his books."

"If it's books you want, I can help," Talia said. "Follow me."

The friends followed Talia along a hallway until they reached a small door. It was carved out of the stone wall. Talia ducked down and walked through it. Tag followed, and his feathers brushed the top of the door.

They entered another hallway that looked like a tunnel. It was dark, damp, and cold, and Talia's and Blaze's heads almost touched the ceiling. Torches hung from the wall. Talia ruffled her feathers, and they lit up one by one, lighting the way.

They walked until the path broke into two directions. One went to the right, and one went to the left. Talia chose the left.

"What is down the other path?" Claw asked as they followed her down the tunnel.

"That path is closed," Talia replied. "No one can go down there."

"Why?" Claw asked.

"It is said to hold great danger," Talia replied.

The tunnel widened as they walked, until . . .

"Wow!" Blaze gasped.

Tag's beak hung open in surprise. They were in a gigantic room, full of shelves stacked with books. It was just like Grey's library but much bigger.

"It's wonderful!" Skyla said.

Talia nodded. "These books contain all of our firehawk history. It could be a good place to search for clues about magical objects." Then she left the friends alone.

Tag gazed around at the thousands of books and scrolls. He felt a bit dizzy.

It could take years to search through all these books, he thought. How would they ever find what they were looking for?

THE LIBRARY

The four friends spent all day in the library. Tag, Blaze, and Claw searched through the higher shelves. Skyla looked through scrolls on the floor.

"We've been here forever, and we've found nothing!" Tag grumbled.

"Look at this book," Blaze replied. "It has some interesting things about my family. And about the Owls of Valor in Perodia too."

Skyla, Tag, and Claw came over to listen.

"Since the beginning of time, the Owls of Valor and the firehawks have worked together," Blaze read.

Tag sighed. His heart felt sad at the thought of the Owls of Valor. It was his dream to become one someday and protect Valor Wood. *If we can't find a magical object*, he thought, *I might never become an Owl of Valor.*

"The Owls of Valor protected the first firehawk egg," Blaze continued.

Skyla wrinkled her nose. "What was the *first* firehawk egg?" she asked.

"I've never heard of it," Tag added.

Blaze read on. "All firehawk eggs are magical, but the first firehawk egg is the most magical of them all. After the first firehawk hatched, the egg shell didn't turn to ash. Instead, it repaired itself and became filled with the most powerful magic in the world. But like all magic, this egg could be used for good *or* for evil."

Tag shivered. He knew what terrible things evil magic like The Shadow could do.

Skyla gasped and pointed to the bottom of the page. "Some say that the first egg could open a permanent portal between lands," she read.

Tag jumped into the air. "This is what we've been looking for!" he cried.

"We could use the egg to open a portal and get home!" Claw added.

But Blaze shook her head as she read on. "The first egg was lost hundreds of years ago. Nobody knows where it is now."

Tag put his head in his wings.

Blaze patted his shoulder. "I'm sorry," she whispered. "We'll come back tomorrow and keep reading. I know we'll find a way to open a portal."

They walked back to the temple and found the great hall. The tables were piled high with delicious food and drinks.

Tag's tummy growled.

"Feeling hungry?" Skyla laughed.

They sat with Talia. And Tag ate until he felt like he might burst.

When Tag, Skyla, Blaze, and Claw had all finished eating, Talia took them to a large beach hut.

"You can stay here," she said. "For as long as you need to. Good night."

The hut was full of snuggly blankets and soft cushions. In the center was a bowl of nuts and fruit.

"You can never have too many nuts," Skyla said. She grabbed a few and tucked them into her armor.

The friends curled up on the cushions. But they were too soft for Tag to sleep on, so he went outside. He gathered some long leaves from a palm tree and made a nest on the beach. As he lay down, he noticed a dark figure sneaking away from their hut. The bright moon suddenly peeked out from behind a cloud. Light shone down onto the figure. Tag gasped.

It was Claw!

THE MAZE

T ag jumped up and chased after Claw. *Where is he going?* Tag wondered.

Claw entered the Golden Temple. Tag quietly followed behind him. Soon, Claw reached the small door and disappeared down the hallway.

Tag waited a moment, then followed him.

Claw took a lit torch from the wall and used it to light the way. Tag followed behind.

He watched as Claw reached the split in the path. But instead of taking the path on the left, which led to the library, Claw turned right!

Why is Claw going down the path that Talia said was dangerous? Tag wondered.

He was curious what Claw was up to, but he didn't want to go into the tunnel alone.

Tag raced back to the hut. He woke Blaze and Skyla and explained where Claw had gone.

Blaze shook her head slowly. "My mom said that no one is allowed down that path."

"I know," Tag replied. "But what if Claw found out there's a magical object down there? We should search *everywhere*."

Skyla and Blaze exchanged a nervous look. "Okay," Blaze finally said.

The friends ran back to the tunnel. They quickly reached the entrance to the closed pathway. It was pitch black.

"I'm not sure this is a good idea," Skyla said.

"Blaze will keep us safe," Tag said.

Blaze didn't look so sure, but she ruffled her feathers to light up the tunnel.

Tag took a deep breath, and they headed down the dangerous path.

LOST!

"Claw?" Tag called out.

There was no reply.

"CLAW!" he called again with a shaky voice. But only his echo replied:

Claw . . . Claw . . . Claw.

There was a sudden loud scraping noise.

"What is that?" Skyla whispered.

Blaze's feathers grew brighter, and Skyla squealed. The walls were moving!

Tag turned around, but a new wall blocked the way back to the entrance.

"That wall wasn't there before!" Tag cried.

"This place is a maze. A magical maze!" Blaze yelled.

The walls moved left and right. Then a wall moved right in front of Skyla—and blocked her behind it!

"Tag!" Skyla cried. "Blaze!"

Tag pressed his wings against the wall, trying to move it.

Skyla was trapped on the other side!

"Blaze!" Tag cried. "Use your fireballs. Maybe they could blast a hole in the wall."

Tag moved back, waiting for a fireball to fly past him, but nothing happened. There was another loud scraping noise.

Suddenly, everything went dark.

"Blaze?" Tag said. He turned around.

But another wall had appeared behind Tag, blocking him from Blaze.

Tag touched the wall. His heart was thumping. "Blaze!" he called.

"I can see a path!" Blaze shouted through the wall. "I'm going to follow it. Maybe it will lead me out of the maze so I can go get help."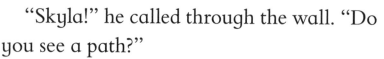

"Okay," Tag replied. He ran to where Skyla was trapped.

"Skyla!" he called through the wall. "Do you see a path?"

"I think so," Skyla said. Her voice sounded quiet behind the wall.

"Follow the path," Tag told her. "I'll find another way to reach you."

There was a loud scraping noise again. The wall beside Tag moved . . . and revealed a new path! He raced down it.

After a while, he stopped for a rest and shouted out to his friends. "Blaze! Skyla! Can you hear me?"

But there was no reply.

Why did I make them come down this path with me? Tag thought. *I should have listened to Talia. It is too dangerous here!*

He thought of his friend Coralie, the seal who had been lost in the Crystal Caverns until Tag, Skyla, and Blaze had rescued her. Tag felt very alone.

He put his head in his wings, when suddenly—

SCRITCH! SCRATCH! RUMBLE RUMBLE!

He sat up and listened. Something was moving through the maze.

SCRITCH! SCRATCH! RUMBLE RUMBLE!

The sound was getting closer. It was too loud to be Skyla or Blaze.

SCRITCH! SCRATCH! RUMBLE RUMBLE!

And it was heading right for Tag!

THE MONSTER

Tag flew as fast as he could, swooping this way and that. He could hear something moving behind him, getting closer and closer. He turned his head and saw a large creature! It was furry like a caterpillar, with yellow and green stripes. It had four horns on its head, and its long body was so wide that it took up the whole tunnel.

It's going to catch me! Tag thought. Then he remembered his gift from Talia.

Blaze's mother had given Tag and Skyla each a special gift. Tag's was a bright green liquid that swirled inside a small glass bottle that hung from around his neck. The liquid gave him magical flying powers, but only for a short amount of time.

He quickly opened the bottle and let a drop of the magical liquid drip into his beak.

Suddenly, his wings began to flap. They flapped faster and faster—so fast he could barely see them! Tag zoomed through the maze and grinned back at the giant caterpillar as it chased after him.

After a while, Tag's wings started to slow down. Then he heard a new, *louder* noise. It sounded like thunder! Tag looked back.

The caterpillar was still behind him. But now there was something else chasing the caterpillar. It was a gigantic marble!

It's going to squish us both! Tag realized in terror.

The caterpillar reached Tag.

"Jump onto my back!" the caterpillar shouted.

Tag didn't have time to think. He grabbed the caterpillar's fur, and they raced on as the marble rumbled behind them. The marble was gaining speed!

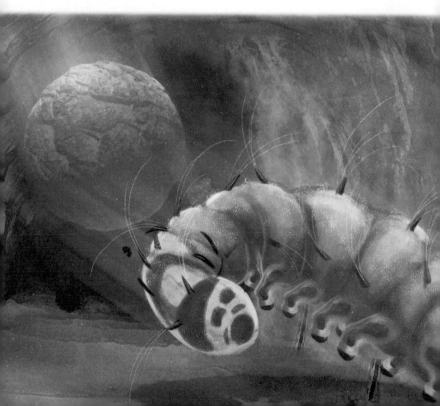

But then Tag could see the path ahead of them was ending. And beyond it was nothing but a deep black hole.

"Stop!" Tag yelled. He closed his eyes and waited for them to fall.

RESCUE!

Tag held his breath. They weren't falling. They were *flying*! He opened his eyes. They were soaring over the hole!

"Hold on!" the caterpillar yelled. There was nothing below them but darkness.

Tag hugged the caterpillar tight until they landed on the other side of the hole with a huge **BUMP!** Tag fell onto the ground. His heart was pounding.

"Look!" the caterpillar said.

Tag watched as the massive marble reached the end of the path on the other side. It fell down, down, down, into the hole.

"How deep do you think that hole is?" Tag asked.

The caterpillar shivered. "I don't know. And I never want to find out."

Tag turned to face the caterpillar. "Thank you for saving me," he said. "I'm Tag."

The caterpillar gave Tag a wide smile. "I'm Charlie."

"Are you lost in this maze, too?" Tag asked.

The caterpillar yawned loudly, then shook his head. "I have lived in the maze for a very, very long time," he said. "But the maze has always been still and quiet. Until now, that is."

"I wonder why it woke up?" Tag said.

He suddenly remembered Skyla, Blaze, and Claw.

"My friends are lost!" he cried. "A squirrel, a firehawk, and a vulture. Have you seen them?"

Charlie shook his head. "I haven't seen anyone in this maze for a very long time," he said.

"I have to find my friends. They might be in trouble. Do you know the way out of here?" Tag asked.

"I've never left the maze, so I'm not sure," Charlie said. "But I'll try to help you."

He slid off into a dark tunnel, and Tag followed. Then Charlie gasped!

Bright orange and red and yellow lights sparkled all around them. The tunnel exploded with fireworks!

THE FIRST
FIREHAWK EGG

"Those are Blaze's lights!" Tag cried.
"She's showing us the way."

"Pretty!" Charlie said.

Tag and Charlie followed Blaze's magical
fireworks.

36

"I've never seen lights like these before," Charlie said. His eyes were wide.

"Wait until you see what else Blaze can do," Tag told him.

The tunnel became brighter and brighter. Tag heard familiar voices talking.

"Skyla!" he cried. "Blaze!"

He turned the corner and crashed into Skyla.

"You found us!" she said, hugging him hard.

"I knew it would work." Blaze grinned. She waved her wings, and more tiny lights floated into the air.

"Look who else we found," Skyla said.

Claw stepped out of the shadows behind her.

"Claw!" Tag said. "Why did you come down this dangerous path on your own?"

Claw looked at the ground. "I thought there might be a magical object down here," he replied.

He spotted Charlie, and his eyes widened. "Who is that creature?!" Claw cried, and leaped in front of Skyla to protect her.

Tag held his wings up. "This is my new friend, Charlie. He helped me find you."

"Hello!" Charlie said cheerfully, waving his legs.

"I'm so sorry," Tag said to his friends. "Talia was right—this place is dangerous."

Blaze nodded. "Yes. But Claw was right," she said. "There *is* something hidden down here."

She led them into a small cavern.

It glowed with a bright blue light. Tag shaded his eyes with his wing as he followed Blaze.

In the center of the room was a large, flat rock. On top of it sat an egg. It was twice the size of the egg that Blaze had hatched from, and it glowed. Hundreds of tiny blue sparks flashed inside it.

"What are those blue sparks?" Tag asked.

"They're pure magic," Blaze replied.

"The first firehawk egg," Claw whispered. His eyes glowed as they reflected the blue light from the egg. "The most powerful magical object in the world."

Skyla looked at Tag. "Your sack is glowing!" she cried.

Tag gasped. He opened his sack. Inside, the Ember Stone was glowing with the same blue light as the egg. He had never seen it glow *blue* before!

He carefully touched the stone. "It feels cool," he said, frowning. "Usually the Ember Stone glows hot."

Tag lifted it out of his sack. Blue light shot out from the egg—right into the Ember Stone. The Ember Stone glowed even brighter as it filled up with tiny blue sparks.

"Wow!" Tag cried.

"I think the magic from the egg has given the Ember Stone its powers back," Skyla said.

Blaze laughed. "This egg is the magical object that will get you three home!"

MAGIC

The friends all hugged each other. Claw joined in too, even though he hated hugs. Skyla whooped and jumped up and down. Tag could see tears in her eyes.

"Should we try to open a portal now?" Tag asked.

Blaze looked at the magic swirling inside the egg and inside the Ember Stone. "I'm not sure," she said. "I almost lost control when I used the Ember Stone to defeat Thorn. And this egg could be even more powerful than the stone. What if something goes wrong?"

Skyla held Blaze's wing. "Blaze is right. We should tell Talia what we've found. She will know what to do."

A small beam of light lit the path ahead. "I think that light might be a way out," Charlie said.

Charlie started to follow it. They followed after him until the light became very bright and they found an opening in the wall.

"Thank you, Charlie," Tag said. "You saved my life." He gave Charlie a hug.

Charlie grinned. "Maybe you can come back and visit me someday?" he asked.

"We'd like that," Tag said. He waved as Charlie wriggled back into the maze.

The friends stepped out into bright light. The sun shone above them.

"We're back on the beach!" Skyla said. She pointed to their hut ahead of them.

Tag watched the baby firehawks playing on the sand. Claw walked away down the beach, past a nest of new firehawk eggs.

"I'll miss this place," Tag said.

Skyla nodded. "Me too," she said.

"Let's find my mom," Blaze said.

They raced off and found Talia walking along the beach. She laughed when they all started to talk at once.

"Slow down!" she said. "Tell me what has happened."

"The first egg," Blaze puffed. "We found it . . . in the maze."

Talia blinked. "What maze?"

"The egg is . . . down the closed path," Tag said. He stared at the sand.

Talia was quiet for a moment.

"Well," she said finally. "What you did was very dangerous. You could have been hurt." She gave them a stern stare. "But I'm glad you found the egg. I always thought it might be hidden somewhere in the Land of the Firehawks. And with the egg, you are no longer trapped here."

"So we can open a portal?" Blaze asked. "My friends can go home?"

Talia smiled, then nodded.

Blaze looked at Tag and Skyla with tears in her eyes.

"Why are you sad?" Talia asked.

Tag sniffed. He knew how Blaze felt. He didn't want to say goodbye.

"Wait!" Skyla said. "The book from the library said that the egg could open a *permanent* portal!"

Blaze jumped up. "We could open a door between here and Perodia that stays open forever!"

A NEW PORTAL

The friends quickly found Claw and returned to the tunnel with Talia. They turned right down the closed path to enter the maze.

"Be careful," Blaze warned. "The maze is magical. The walls move, so we must stick together."

Talia lit up her feathers, and Blaze did the same. "I'm ready," Talia said.

But as they walked along the twisty, winding paths, the walls stayed still.

As they neared the cavern, they saw that the blue light was shining stronger than ever.

"I don't think we need our light anymore," Blaze said. Her feathers went dull.

They entered the cavern. Talia gasped as she saw the egg. "It's more wonderful than I ever imagined," she said.

"Now see if you can open a portal, Blaze," Skyla said.

Blaze looked at her friends and paused.

"You can do it," Tag told her. "I know you can. You're stronger than ever." He looked to her new magical silver tail feather.

Blaze smiled and held out her wing. Very slowly, she picked up the Ember Stone and then touched the egg.

A burst of blue light surrounded Blaze. It turned her feathers sparkly blue. They looked like ocean waves. The magic rippled through Blaze's feathers. Her eyes went wide. "It's amazing!" she said. "I can feel the magic flowing through me."

"Concentrate," Talia told Blaze. "Try to control the magic. See if you can open a portal."

Tag watched Blaze. His friend's eyes narrowed as she focused on the egg.

"Do you think this will work?" Skyla whispered to Tag.

Tag squeezed Skyla's paw. "If anyone can do it, Blaze can," he said.

Claw squawked beside them. "It's working! Look!"

The wall began shimmering. Tag could see the outline of a door appearing. As the magic began to die down, the door turned solid and golden. This portal was different from the others they had opened. Those portals weren't solid.

Then Blaze's feathers turned back to their normal color, and the egg's blue light dimmed.

"You did it, Blaze!" Talia said. She hugged her daughter. "You have opened a permanent portal to Perodia."

Skyla whooped and joined in the hug. "Come on!" she said to Tag.

Tag joined in too, then grabbed Claw's wing and pulled him into the giant hug.

Tag grinned at Claw, and the vulture smiled back. "We can go home," Claw said.

"*And* we can all visit Blaze and Talia whenever we want," Skyla added.

"Maybe I will come to Valor Wood sometime," Talia said. "It's been a long time since I've seen my old friend Grey."

"I'm going to come with you to Perodia," Blaze told them. "I'd like to see Grey and the Owls of Valor."

Blaze gave Talia a hug. "I'll be back soon," she said. She turned to her friends. "Ready?"

"Let's go home," Tag said. He waved goodbye to Talia, then held his breath.

The friends held on to each other's wings and paws and stepped through the portal.

CHAPTER 10

RETURN TO PERODIA

Tag and his friends were suddenly sliding down a twisty see-through tunnel. Lots of different colors whizzed past: red, orange, blue, green, and purple.

"Wow!" Tag yelled.

"Woo-hoo! Skyla cried in front of him.

"This is so much fun!" Blaze shouted.

Claw made a moaning sound behind Tag. "I feel sick," he said.

Tag didn't feel so good either. His tummy felt wobbly, and his head felt dizzy.

He could see through the tunnel walls. Tag shivered as they passed over twisty thorn bushes.

"The Shadowlands," Claw whispered behind him.

They traveled quickly, and before long, beautiful blue water sparkled below them. "I see the nixies!" Blaze called.

Tag waved as they sped past Lullaby Lake, but the nixies couldn't see them.

They zoomed on, sliding through the tunnel. The air became cold. Tag's breath puffed up in clouds in front of him. All around, everything was bright white. Something shimmered and sparkled ahead. *The Crystal Caverns*, Tag thought.

A buzzing noise surrounded them, and Tag knew where they were heading past next.

"Grumblebees!" Tag laughed.

The grumblebees swarmed around a meadow filled with flowers. They were playing with two large bears. In the distance, Tag could see the Whispering Oak. *We must almost be home*, he thought.

The air warmed again, and they traveled over the waves of the Blue Bay until they saw a small island with a volcano on it.

"Fire Island!" Skyla shouted. "The tunnel is taking us back to where we started."

Tag opened his beak to speak, when he suddenly flew out of the tunnel! He landed in a pile of soft sand.

"We're home!" Skyla yelled. She brushed sand from her fur. "We're finally home!"

"*Almost* home," Claw said. He picked up a sack that Tag hadn't seen before. "We're in Perodia, but we still need to return to Valor Wood. I have to finish what I started."

Tag frowned. "What do you mean?" he asked.

Claw didn't answer. He took to the sky, headed toward Valor Wood.

Skyla jumped onto Blaze's back, and they flew off after him.

"Come on!" Skyla shouted.

Tag followed his friends. He was excited to get home, and to see Grey again. But something felt wrong. He wasn't sure why, but he had a bad feeling deep in his tummy. *Was it a mistake to come back to Perodia?* he wondered.

THE OWLS
OF VALOR

They flew closer and closer to Valor Wood. The closer they flew, the more fluttery Tag's tummy felt.

The air was fresh and sweet. He could hear a stream tinkling in the distance, and his heart felt full.

He was home.

Tag and Blaze landed beside Claw at the edge of the trees. Skyla looked even more excited to be home than Tag. She hopped from foot to foot with a huge grin on her face.

A loud noise filled the air.

TA-RAAAAAAA! TA-RAAAAAA!

It was the Owls of Valor's horns.

"They are welcoming us home!" Tag called to his friends.

"Look!" Blaze said. She pointed to the sky.

The Owls of Valor swooped down over the trees, led by Maximus. They were wearing their shiny armor, and they held sharp swords and shields. With them was Grey, their leader.

Grey landed in front of Tag. Tag gave him a huge smile, but Grey didn't smile back.

"Tag, Skyla, Blaze! " Maximus shouted. "Move behind me."

Tag frowned at Skyla. She looked just as confused as he did.

"What's wrong, Grey?" Tag asked.

Grey pointed a wing at Claw, who stood beside them.

"You are banished from Valor Wood, Thorn," Grey said. "Leave at once!"

"It's okay," Tag started. "He's not Thorn. He's—"

Claw looked to Tag, and an evil grin stretched across his face.

"Grey is right," Claw said, looking directly at Tag. "I *am* Thorn."

BETRAYED!

The vulture laughed a horrible, cruel laugh.

"No!" cried Skyla.

"Yes!" Thorn said. "I followed you through the portal into the Cloud Kingdom. I knew I couldn't reach the Land of the Firehawks without you, so I pretended I was Claw. You took my Shadow from me, and now I have taken something from you."

He reached into his sack and pulled out a firehawk egg. A *stolen* firehawk egg!

"All firehawk eggs are magical in some way. This egg will help me get my evil powers back. And you three *helped* me do it!" He gave them a slow, twisted smile.

"We trusted you! " Blaze shouted. Her feathers lit up one by one, and she held out a glowing fireball.

"Give us the egg back, Claw," Tag said. "Please."

The vulture frowned. "I told you," he said. "I am not Claw. I am Thorn."

Tag took a step closer to Thorn.

"Why did you help us?" Tag asked. "You saved us from the croco-dragon. You saved Skyla from the poisoned flower. You helped Blaze find her family, and us to find a way home."

Thorn shook his head. "I needed you to trust me so I could get the egg. That's all."

Skyla stood beside Tag. "You didn't have to save me, though," she said. "You didn't need *me* in order to find the egg."

Blaze lowered the fireball. "You were our friend," she said sadly.

Grey held up his sword. "Thorn is *nobody's* friend. Owls of Valor, attack!"

Grey and the Owls of Valor swooped toward Thorn.

Skyla and Blaze looked at Tag. "What should we do?" they asked.

"I don't want to hurt a friend," Blaze said.

"He's not our friend anymore. And we have to get that egg back!" Tag said. He pulled out his dagger and ran at Thorn.

Thorn glared at Tag. Twirling, swirling black smoke circled him, and then **POOF!** He was gone.

CHAPTER 13

THE STOLEN EGG

"Where did Thorn go?" asked Tag.

"He is probably on his way back to The Shadowlands," Skyla replied.

Blaze nodded.

"You are correct," Grey said. "But Thorn is dangerous. I will send my Owls of Valor to find him—and the egg."

Tag lowered his head. "He tricked us," he said. "We thought he was our friend. It is *our* responsibility to make it right and get the egg back."

Skyla patted Tag's wing. "I don't think he was tricking us all the time," she said. "I think Thorn *did* want to be our friend."

Blaze went to Grey. "Let us go after him," she said. "I know we can get the egg back. Then I will return it to my home."

Grey's eyes widened. "You found your family?" he asked.

Blaze smiled. "I found my mother in the Land of the Firehawks."

"And Blaze used the first firehawk's egg to open a permanent portal!" Skyla added.

Grey's eyes grew even wider. "There is a lot you need to tell me," he said. "But for now, we must get that egg back."

Maximus, the Captain of the Owls of Valor, stepped forward. "We are ready to fight Thorn," he said. He held up his sword and shield.

"Please, Grey," Tag said. "Let us go alone first and see if we can get the egg."

Grey looked at Tag, Skyla, and Blaze.

"You three have been on a long journey," Grey said. "You must be tired. But you have also done things that no other creature in the wood could do."

"You have been braver than I thought you could be," Maximus admitted.

"If you think you can get the egg back from Thorn, then I trust you," Grey

continued. "I will give you a head start. But if you fail, the Owls of Valor will destroy Thorn once and for all."

Tag gulped, then nodded. He didn't know how they were going to get the egg back, or how much evil magic Thorn still had. But he knew they had to try.

Tag looked at his friends. "Are you ready for one last adventure?" he asked them.

Skyla grinned and held out her slingshot. Blaze lit up her feathers and sent out hundreds of tiny glowing fireballs into the sky.

"Let's go get that egg back!" Tag said.

SECOND CHANGES

The friends flew quickly to The Shadowlands. They landed in a small clearing that was surrounded by thorny bushes. The ground was gray and dusty, and everything was brown.

Tag pulled out his dagger, and Skyla held up her slingshot.

Blaze looked to the sky for tiger bats, but it was empty.

They heard a rustle coming from the bushes. Tag spun around and held his dagger tightly.

"I know you're there, Thorn!" Tag called.

"I have no army," Thorn said as he came out of the bushes. "My spies left when you destroyed my Shadow."

"Is that why you stole the egg?" Blaze asked. "To get your Shadow back?"

Tag and Skyla looked at each other. They lowered their weapons.

Thorn looked at Blaze. "The Shadow was always there for me," he said.

"What about your spies?" Skyla said.

Thorn looked sad. "My spies were only under my spell."

Just then, Tag realized something. "The Shadow was your only friend," he said.

Thorn nodded.

"But *we* were your friends," Skyla said.

"You don't have to be evil anymore," Blaze added. She stepped closer.

"We are *still* your friends, Thorn," Tag told him. "But you have to give us the egg."

Thorn turned to Skyla, Tag, and Blaze. Slowly, he started to smile.

TA-RAAAAAAA! TA-RAAAAAA!

Tag looked to the sky.

Hundreds of Owls of Valor swooped down, led by Maximus and Grey.

"Do you have the egg?" Grey asked Tag.

Tag sadly shook his head. "Please!" he said, turning to Thorn and holding out his wing.

"I'm sorry, Tag, but we can't let Thorn destroy Perodia," Grey said.

"Thorn has changed!" Blaze cried. "He is not the evil vulture he used to be."

Thorn lifted his wings. Dark smoke began to twirl around him. "Grey will always see me as the enemy," Thorn said.

"Owls of Valor!" Grey called. "Attack!"

THE NEW OWLS
OF VALOR

"**N**o!" cried Tag. He jumped in front of Thorn and faced Grey and the Owls of Valor. Skyla leaped over to join him, and Blaze did the same.

"Thorn did lots of bad things. But he has done good things too. He saved us in the Cloud Kingdom—all of us. And we would never have found Blaze's family without his help. He deserves another chance," Tag said.

"He was banished from Perodia," Grey replied. "He knew what would happen if he returned."

"We don't need to fight again," Tag said. "There is another way." He pulled the Ember Stone from his sack. It glowed with magic. Tag looked at Skyla and Blaze, and they both nodded.

"You can have the Ember Stone," Tag told Thorn. "*If* you return the egg."

"What are you doing, Tag?" Grey cried.

Thorn's eyes grew wide. "Why would you give me the stone after I tricked you?" he asked.

"Show them that you are good, Thorn. Do the right thing," Tag said. He handed Thorn the Ember Stone.

Tag held his breath.

Thorn lifted the stone. Light shot out of it in all directions.

Suddenly, colorful flowers sprouted from the thorny bushes all around them. Green plants grew out of the ground, and yellow butterflies fluttered in the air above.

"It's beautiful!" Blaze said.

Thorn smiled. "It is," he replied. He turned to Grey. "I'm sorry, I don't want to be the evil Thorn anymore. If you'll let me stay in Perodia, I will be Claw and use magic only for good." He handed Blaze the egg.

Grey nodded once at Claw. "If you continue to do good, then you may stay."

He then turned to Tag and Skyla.

Tag gulped. Grey looked very serious. But then he put his wing on Tag's shoulder.

"Tag, you have shown that even the smallest owl can be strong and brave," Grey said. He pulled out a golden medal and put it around Tag's neck. "You are now an Owl of Valor."

"TAG!" Maximus yelled. "You are to report to me in the morning for training. Don't be late!"

Tag grinned, and Maximus gave a small smile back. Tag didn't think he'd ever been so happy in his life. He felt all warm and fuzzy inside. Skyla and Blaze cheered.

"Skyla," Grey continued, "you are fearless and clever. You may not be an owl, but I invite you to also become an Owl of Valor." He placed a medal around Skyla's neck.

Skyla gasped. "Really?" she said. She did a big flip in the air.

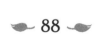

"Blaze," Grey said, "you will be a great leader one day. Please invite Talia and the other firehawks to visit us soon."

"Thank you, Grey." Blaze smiled.

Grey raised his wings to the sky. "Before you head home, Blaze, let us have a feast!" he shouted. "To celebrate our newest Owls of Valor!"

Then Grey leaned down to quietly speak to Tag. "You have come so far, Tag. I am very proud of you," he said, then flew away.

The Owls of Valor followed.

Tag, Skyla, Blaze, and Claw stood in the Shadowlands. Tag smiled.

"You should have this," Claw said, handing Tag the Ember Stone. "I don't need it anymore."

Tag shook Claw's wing. Then he pulled Claw, Skyla, and Blaze into a big hug.

"I can't wait for our next adventure," Tag whispered to his best friends.

ABOUT THE AUTHOR

KATRINA CHARMAN has wanted to be a children's book writer ever since she was eleven, when her teacher asked her class to write an epilogue to Roald Dahl's *Matilda*. Katrina's teacher thought her writing was good enough to send to Roald Dahl himself! Sadly, she never got a reply, but this experience ignited her love of reading and writing. Katrina lives in England with her husband and three children. The Last Firehawk is her first early chapter book series in the U.S.

ABOUT THE ILLUSTRATOR

JUDIT TONDORA was born in Hungary and now works from her countryside studio. Her illustrations are rooted in the traditional European style but also contain elements of American mainstream style. Her characters have a vivacious retro vibe placed right into the present day: she says, "I put the good old retro together with modern style to give charisma to my illustrations."

The LAST FIREHAWK
The Secret Maze

Questions and Activities

1. **R**eread page 13. What special power does the first firehawk egg have? Why do the friends want to find the egg?

2. **T**ag, Skyla, and Blaze get separated in the underground maze. What is magical about the maze? How do the friends find each other again?

3. **A**s Tag travels through the portal, he looks out at the different parts of Perodia. Where in Perodia would *you* most like to visit? What would you like to do there?

4. **C**law stole a firehawk egg so he could get The Shadow back. Why does he want The Shadow? What are two words that describe how you think Claw feels in this moment?

5. **W**hat adventure do you think Tag, Skyla, Blaze, and Claw will have next? Write a paragraph that imagines their next adventure.